604335

ABOUT THE AUTHOR

D.J. Lucas

always wanted to be a writer. Today D.J. is one of
the most popular children's authors around.
D.J.'s books include *My Teacher's a Nutcase*,
winner of the Smartstart Award and *I Dare You*,
winner of the Bitread Book Award.

Sally Grindley

the acclaimed children's writer, is D.J.'s favourite
author. Sally Grindley says, 'I would do anything
to write as well as D.J. Lucas, even lock myself in
a cupboard with NO biscuits to eat!'

Visit Sally Grindley's website: www.sallygrindley.co.uk

ORCHARD BOOKS
338 Euston Road, London NW1 3BH
Hachette Children's Books Australia
Level 17/207 Kent Street, Sydney NSW 2000
ISBN-10: 1 84616 085 5
ISBN-13: 978 1 84616 085 1
First published in 2006 by Orchard Books
Text © Sally Grindley 2006
Illustrations © Tony Ross 2006
The rights of Sally Grindley to be identified as the author and of Tony Ross
to be identified as the illustrator of this work have been asserted by them
in accordance with the Copyright, Designs and Patents Act, 1988.
A CIP catalogue record for this book is available from the British Library.
1 3 5 7 9 10 8 6 4 2
Printed in Great Britain
Orchard Books is a division of Hachette Children's Books

Relax Max

BY D.J. LUCAS

AKA SALLY GRINDLEY

ORCHARD BOOKS

To my friend Max

D.J.

Dear D.J.,

This is the third year we'll be writing to each other, and you're still my favourite author. Can you believe it?! I bet I'm still your greatest fan.

I still think it's amazing that you went on safari for Christmas. Did you see any elephants? You should write about elephants in your next book. They were my dad's favourite animal. Did you know they can pick up a needle with their trunk?

It was brilliant being in *The Wizard of Oz*. James says I was the best Munchkin he's ever seen. He's still Mum's boyfriend. He's quite funny sometimes. Not as funny as Dad was, but quite funny. He hasn't grown his yukky beard again, thank goodness. I didn't like him when he was a hairychops.

Write soon and tell me what animals you saw on safari. GRRRR!

Love, Max

11th January

Dear Max,

How time flies! It doesn't seem like two years
have gone by since you first wrote to me. You'll
have left school and I'll be collecting my
pension soon! I am very honoured that
I am still your favourite author and you are
still, of course, my best fan.

Christopher and I had a wonderful time in
South Africa, and I am now a wildlife expert
(well, I know a lot more than I did). We saw
elephants (wonderful), lions (magnificent),
a leopard (lucky us!), zebra (lots), wildebeest
(hundreds), mongooses (cute), hippos (not
much more than eyeballs), hyenas (ugh!),
vultures (yuk!) and warthogs (ridiculous!).

I was exhausted after four days of trying to sleep in a tent with wild animals snuffling around outside (I dread to think what they were!) and getting up at dawn to go on safari. But I can't wait to go again. It's the most exhilarating thing I've ever done.

Congratulations on being the best Munchkin ever.

Love D.J.

Dear D.J.,

I'm back at school – BIG GROAN! – and guess
what? There are four people shorter than me
in my class now. I'm overtaking everyone!
James says it's because I eat like a horse, but
I said that I've never eaten grass in my life
(joke). I like sugar lumps though.

Mr Hatch (Eggy) is still my teacher, and Ben
and Emily are still my best friends. Jenny
doesn't speak to me any more, but I don't
care because she isn't very nice. We've got
a football match on Saturday. Mum and James
are coming to watch so I hope I play well.

Have you started your new book yet? What's it
going to be about? We're doing poetry at

school this term. Do you ever write any poems?

Love, Max

P.S. Marshmallow babysits a lot now because Mum and James go out a lot. She's so funny, D.J. She wears shoes with ENORMOUS heels, she's got her eyebrows, nose and ears pierced, and she's got the longest scarf I've ever seen. She knitted it herself! She knows millions of card games, so she's teaching me to play them.

20th January

Dear Max,

I can't tell you what my new book is going to be about, because I haven't a clue! My publisher is desperate for me to come up with an idea, but my brain has frozen. I think it's because of all the fuss over *My Teacher's a Nutcase* and *My Teacher's a Fruitcake*. It's scared all the ideas away.

I'm so glad that you're growing so fast. You deserve to after all the prodding about your consultant, Mr Poo, put you through. You'll soon be looking down on Eggy and patting him on the head.

Love D.J.

P.S. I used to write lots of poetry when I was a teenager, but I haven't recently. Poetry-writing is very different from story-writing. With poetry you have to condense all your thoughts into a tiny number of words and encourage your reader to find the meaning in the gaps. Yikes! That makes it sound terribly complicated. It can be, but in its simplest form it can also be huge fun.

25th January

Oh dear, D.J.,

World-famous author doesn't know what to write about! What would the newspapers say if they knew?!

I've had an idea which you might like. I thought you could do a third book about your teacher, and you could call it *My Teacher's a Screwball*. That's an American expression so it might help you sell lots of books in America. What do you think?

We won our football match 5-0 and I scored two goals for the first time ever. Even Huge

Bigbottom said well done, and he usually ignores me. I'll have to make sure Mum and James come to all my matches to give me good luck.

Perhaps you could do a book of poems if you can't think of a story to write.

Love, Max

P.S. James comes to our house a lot now. I like playing computer games with him because he's rubbish – NOT AS BAD AS MUM! – and I always beat him. I like him to show me how to make my drawings better because he's really good at that. But he tries to sit next to Mum on the sofa so I try and get there first, and he gets all kissy kissy with her in the kitchen when he thinks I'm not looking. Yuk! I don't think grown-ups should be allowed to kiss.

2nd February

Dear Two-Goal Max

Gosh, no more kissing for grown-ups. Christopher and I might have something to say about that!

It sounds as if you get on well with James really. It's good that he spends time with you – especially if you insist upon trouncing him at computer games. I bet I'm worse at them than James or your mum. In race games I usually crash before I've even reached the starting line. In fact computers are a complete mystery to me. I've just about mastered word-processing, and that's it.

Well done in the football, Max. That's

fantastic. I bet James was impressed, especially since he's no good at sport.

Love D.J.

P.S. Thank you for your idea for my next book, but I suspect the title might be somewhat unacceptable in England! I'm not planning to write any more *My Teacher* stories. I've run out of mad things for her to do, and it's all become rather confused since the film version turned her into a man.

Dear D.J.,

It's Valentine's Day next week. I'm going to send Emily a card with a limerick in it. We've been doing limericks in class. They have five lines. The last line rhymes with the first two and the middle two rhyme with each other. It's really difficult to think of words that rhyme with each other.

This is what I've written.

Emily is a young girl
With the longest hair in the world
It smells real nice
of sugar and spice
And ends with a beautiful curl

It's a bit soppy but I think Emily will like it. I bet

you get loads of Valentine cards from all your fans. I only get one, and that's from Mum. I always send her one too, and I expect James will as well this year. I hope Emily sends me one.

Love, Max

12th February

Dear Max,

You've mastered the limerick already.
Lucky Emily!

I used to love making up limericks, they're
such fun. How about this one (which I didn't
make up).

There was an old man from Blackheath
Who sat on his set of false teeth
He cried with a start
Oh Lord, bless my heart,
I've bitten myself underneath

I had some great news today, Max, which
I hope will jumpstart my brain again. My

Teacher's a Nutcase has now sold half a million copies and, because the film did so well, they want to make a film of *My Teacher's a Fruitcake*. I'm walking on air! Christopher says never mind jumpstarting my brain, my head will soon be too big for my body (the rotter!).

Love D.J.

P.S. I never receive more than one Valentine card, and I assume that comes from Christopher.

Dear D.J.,

I can't believe they're going to turn *My Teacher's a Fruitcake* into a film as well. I can't wait to see Tom Trews as the teacher and Jennifer Aniseed as the caretaker again. Does that mean I'll be getting another postcard from Hollywood?!

I got TWO Valentine cards. I hope one was from Emily. Mum got two cards as well, one from  me and one from James (he told me). He's taking Mum out for a romantic meal tonight, which is a pain because I like to have Mum to myself for Valentine's. I think he really loves my mum, but not as much as I do. He buys her

things, and sometimes he cooks for us. My dad
was the best though.

Love, Max

P.S. Thank you for the limerick. I showed it to
Eggy and he read it out to my class. They all
thought it was funny.

P.P.S. Huge Bigbottom scored a goal on
Saturday, so I said well done to him.

Dear D.J.,

Guess what, guess what, guess what? Uncle
Twinkletoes Derek and Pauline are going to
have a baby! I'm going to have a little cousin.
It's already ten weeks old and Pauline doesn't
want to know if it's a boy or girl because she
says it's more fun to have a surprise at the
end. If it's a girl, I think they should call it
Emily, and if it's a boy they should call it
Ben. It's going to be born on the 17th
September – CAN YOU BELIEVE THAT?!!!
We'll have birthdays three days
running – Baby
Twinkletoes' on the
17th, mine on the 18th,
and yours on the 19th!
Uncle Derek and

Pauline came round to tell us last night and
Scallywag ran off with one of my slippers.

I still can't find it.

Love, Max

P.S. I wrote a limerick.

There's a baby in Pauline's belly,
At the moment it's just like jelly,
When it's born it will bellow,
Its poo will be yellow,
And its nappies will be all smelly.

Mum turned her nose up, but Ben laughed
when I showed it to him.

Dear Max

That's great news about your Uncle Derek and Pauline. Say congratulations from me.

You've certainly got the limerick bug'!

I think I have the germ of an idea for my new book, so I must try to fertilise it before it goes off.!

Love D.J.

17th February

Dear D.J.,

Grandad and Gran are
coming to stay next
week. It's going to be
Grandad's seventieth
birthday Mum's making
him a cake in the
shape of the number
70 – which means

there are two cakes. (All the more for
me!). Uncle Derek and Pauline are going to
come round, and we're going to have a party.
James has been helping me to make a 'Happy
Birthday' banner with lots of drawings on it,
and then I'm going to make my own card. (I'm
going to do a picture of Grandad fishing,
because that's what he likes best. He'll be

catching an enormous fish weighing 70lb.) I'm going to write a limerick to go inside.

Love, Max

P.S. James hasn't met Grandad and Gran before. I think he's a bit nervous because they're my dad's mum and dad and he knows he can never replace my dad, not in a million trillion years.

Dear Max

I hope the birthday party goes off with a bang. Lucky Grandad, having one of your special cards

I'm still in the doldrums over the new story. I was working on an idea but it just won't allow itself to take shape, so I'm spending more time twiddling my thumbs and gazing out of the window than writing. Have you written any more limericks that will cheer me up?

Love D.J.

23rd February

Dear D.J.,

There once was an author called D.J.,
Whose ideas had flown right away,
  She thought and she thought,
  But her output was nought,
  (James helped with this line)
Then a bestseller hit her one day!

I can't believe my favourite author is still
struggling to write. Mum says she's sure
inspiration will strike you any minute. So am
I. If not, I'll have to find another author to write
to (only joking ☺).

Love, Max

P.S. Gran and
Grandad arrive
tomorrow. They're

staying for four days so that Mum and James can go away for a weekend. I want to go too, but Mum says she wants to spend some grown-up time with James on her own. I don't like it when she says that because it means I'm not grown-up, but I am grown-up and I've been the man in our house ever since Dad died, Mum's always saying so. He'd better not think he can just take over from me.

24th February

Dear Very Grown-up Max

Thank you for your limerick, which did make
me smile – especially the thought of being hit
by a bestseller! I wish it *was* just a question of
standing there and waiting for a bestseller to
hit you in the face, rather than spending hours
and hours tearing your hair out in front of an
empty piece of paper!

Lucky you, having four days with your
grandparents, especially your grandad, who
sounds a real hoot from what you've told me
before. I hope your gran's cooking has
improved though!

Love D.J.

26th February

Dear D.J.,

Grandad's party was amazing! We played
charades, and Uncle Derek was brilliant at
doing the mimes. Mum got the giggles and
couldn't stop when he acted out *The Wind in
the Willows* (it was a bit rude!). Grandad's
teeth fell out when he blew out the candles
on his cake and Scallywag tried to run off with
them. (I found my slipper behind the
washbasin!) We played this game where you
have to do drawings and your team has to
guess what they are. James and I were on the
same team with Gran and Pauline and we won
by miles, even though Gran didn't guess
anything and kept dozing off (Grandad said it
was because of the sherry).

Love, Max

P.S. This is a copy of my limerick for Grandad.
He thinks it's great and says he's going to have
it framed.

Dear Grandad you're getting quite old
And you still don't do what you're told
Gran says that you're naughtier
Than when you were forty (er!)
But you're well worth your weight
in pure gold.

Dear D.J.,

Grandad took me fishing, but we didn't catch a bean. I asked him if he liked James, and he said that he  seemed like a nice young man. I said that he could never replace Dad. Grandad said that he was sure James wouldn't even think to try, but it was good that he was making Mum happy.

Mum's back now and we've just been out for our meal ON OUR OWN. She had a nice time with James, but said she missed me ENORMOUSLY. Then she told me that she loves James and I went all knotted up inside. I didn't know what to say. It was all quiet between us for ages, until Mum asked what I was thinking. I was thinking that I wished James would go away for ever, because now I'm even more worried that he'll try to take my place, but I said that I bet James didn't love her as much as I do. She said of course not and that James would never try to take my place or Dad's. I wanted to ask her if that meant she would never marry him, but the waiter came up to the table. Mum asked if I wanted a doggy bag to put my pudding in. I said we hadn't got a dog, then we started laughing and couldn't stop. I felt better after that and Mum said I was to stop worrying.

Love, Max

P.S. Gran's cooking is still YUK! She did baked potatoes and we couldn't cut through them she'd cooked them for so long. Grandad's shot across the room.

3rd March

Dear Max,

What a great limerick for your grandad! No wonder he wants to have it framed. You have such a talent for writing, Max. I hope you will keep it going. You're pretty good at drawing as well, lucky you. You could write and illustrate your own books, which is more than I can do. If I don't get writing again soon, I'll have to take up a new career.

I'm glad you're feeling better about your mum and James. Nobody's going to steal your mother from you. Try to enjoy having another person in your life, especially one who is happy to give up his time for you.

Love D.J.

36

Dear D.J.,

James has sold his battered old sports car and bought a brand new hatchback (well, it looks brand new compared to his sports car and it's got a CD player and the windscreen wipers work). I can fit in the back without having my knees round my ears! I think James is sad not to have his sports car anymore. I am a bit too because it was good when he drove fast and the wind blew my hair off. James said I was getting too big for it, and he couldn't expect Mum to drive her car all the time when we go out together.

We're doing haikus at school next week, and Eggy's asked us to find out something about them. So I thought I'd ask you! Can you tell me how to write one? Even better, can you write one to me, please? ☺

Love, Max

P.S. What's happening with the new film?

P.P.S. Huge Bigbottom passes the ball to me at football now. He never did that before.

11th March

Dear Max,

Haikus, eh? They are really quite difficult. You have to write a story in just three lines, with five syllables in the first, seven in the second and five in the last. Oh, and they often have something to do with the seasons in them. Here's my attempt at one.

Spring is in the air
and young Max is writing pomes
but I am struggling

Five out of ten for that one I think. I'm sure Eggy wouldn't be impressed.

How-e-ver... I'M OFF TO HOLLYWOOD

NEXT WEEK! Perhaps that's what I need to inspire me. I'm having a preliminary meeting with all the big bosses – producer, director, screenwriter and so on – to discuss changes to the text (groan – I wish they didn't have to make changes) and additional scenes they might want to put in. No doubt they'll keep me at arms' length after that, but it's nice to be involved at the beginning.

Love D.J.

Dear D.J.,

Ha! Pomes, eh? That's cheating!

You're soooooo lucky going to Hollywood AGAIN. You'll soon be the most famous author on the planet!

You could give up writing books. Uncle Derek says you must be very rich from your first film. Now that you've got another one coming out, you won't ever need to write again so it won't matter if you can't think of anything to write about (!) (Mum says it's rude to tell you that, but anyway you can't stop writing because there won't be anything for me to read!) I've just finished reading *I Dare You* — it's really scary.

I've got to write a haiku for homework.
They're even more difficult than I thought they
would be. I wish I had so much money that
I didn't have to do any more homework ever
again! I could say to Eggy, 'you can't make me
write a haiku because I am very rich and
famous and I don't do things like that unless
I want to – so there'.

Love, Max

Dear Max

Well, here I am again, eating ridiculous amounts of food, and lapping up my few minutes of fame before I'm sent back home to mind my own business. Actually, I feel a bit of a fraud being introduced as a world famous author when at the moment I can't write for toffee. I've nicknamed the producer of the film Humpty Dumpty because his waist is larger than his chest. I thought you'd approve.

Love, D.J.

3D Sharpener St
Any town
MX9 3BT
U.K.

GREETINGS FROM HOLLYWOOD CALIFORNIA

27th March

Dear Max,

I'm back and down to earth with a resounding
bump. My computer screen is staring at me
accusingly, so I keep having to go away to do
other things. The truth is, Max, that a writer
has to write. It's in our blood. Even if I became
the richest person on earth, I would still want
to tell stories. I shall carry on writing until
I can no longer move my fingers over the
keyboard – which I hope won't be for donkeys'
years. Something, eventually, will shift the
current blockage, and off I will go on
a whirling tide of inspiration.

Love D.J.

P.S. They're hoping to cast George Moony as

the alcoholic school governor in the new film. If I meet him, I may never come back down to earth again!

30th March

Dear D.J.,

When I told Mum you might get to meet George Moony she went all swoony. (I'm getting good at poetry!) He's her favourite.

Pauline's baby is sixteen weeks old now and she says her bump is growing bigger by the minute. Uncle Derek keeps patting it and saying 'how's my little fatty?' and Pauline says 'hark who's talking'. She let me pat it once, and it's really hard. I thought it would be soft.

Love, Max

P.S. Thank you for
the postcard. This
is a picture of
your producer.
P.P.S. I'm glad
you're going to
keep on writing.

Dear D.J.,

James and Mum went out last night and Marshmallow babysat. She brought a new game with her to play on the computer. It was so funny, D.J. You had to be a mole and burrow under all these fields and mountains and houses and towns to try and catch worms before the birds got them. Marshmallow caught hundreds more worms than me. (She's been practising.)

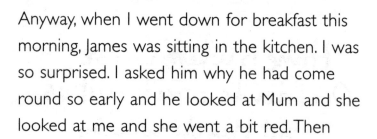

Anyway, when I went down for breakfast this morning, James was sitting in the kitchen. I was so surprised. I asked him why he had come round so early and he looked at Mum and she looked at me and she went a bit red. Then she said that because it had been very late when they got in, James had stayed at our house. I asked him if he had slept on the sofa and that it must have been uncomfortable, but nobody said anything and Mum went red again. Then she said that James had slept in her room and that it was all right because they loved each other. But I didn't want James to sleep with her because they're not married and if they're not married he might still go away.

I didn't want my breakfast, and I went to school so grumpy that I got into trouble with Eggy for answering back.

Love, Max

P.S. I did this haiku.

Home is where we live
Our friends come to visit us
but they do not stay.

7th April

Dear Max,

So many things are changing in your life, I'm not surprised you want to throw your toys out of the pram. It must be especially difficult since you and your mother have lived in your flat together, on your own, for so long. Don't run and hide from things though, Max. Go and talk with your mother and James and tell them exactly how you feel. They won't be happy if they know you're miserable.

I've got a very hectic ten days coming up. I'm doing a tour of Germany, Austria, Spain and Portugal, signing books in bookshops and visiting my overseas publishers. It seems that everyone is desperate to meet me because of the films, and a number of my older books are being reissued with new covers. Having spent years trying to eke out a living from writing, suddenly I don't have to do anything and yet I'm being showered with publicity, invitations, and the chance to meet George Moony.

Love D.J.

Dear D.J.,

You're so lucky visiting all those different
countries. Does it mean I'll have another four
postcards to add to my collection?! You've
already sent me ten since we first started
writing – I counted them when your
Hollywood one arrived.

Mum came home from work yesterday and
said that she wanted to have a serious talk
with me. She said she was sorry she hadn't
told me about James staying, but that they
were committed to each other and that she
had never even considered having another
man in her life until James had come along.
She said that she would never forget Dad, and
that he would always have a place in her
heart, but that she was ready to move on and

find happiness with someone else. She said that she hoped I would accept James into my life as well and that we would be the best of friends.

Ben and Emily are my best friends. I haven't got room for any more.

Love, Max

Dear Max

The puddings here are to die for. I shall turn into a pudding if I keep eating them! I am in a city called Salzburg, where they have one of the greatest puppet theatres in the world. I watched a performance of Peter and the Wolf (shown on the front of this card) and thought how much you would have loved it. It was quite extraordinary, and the wolf puppet was really quite scary.

Love D.J.

SALZBURG
30 12

REPUBLIK ÖSTERREICH

30 Sharpener St.
Anytown
MX9 3BT
V.K.

54

21st April

Dear Max,

I've come back from my tour exhausted, but
I had a wonderful time. I'm afraid I only
managed to send you one postcard though.
I was whisked around so quickly and
surrounded by so many people from dawn
till dusk, that there wasn't the opportunity
to write any more.

Back to staring gormlessly at the computer.

Love D.J.

P.S. I'm receiving so many fan letters now that
I shall have to employ someone to help me
answer them! Don't worry – I'll always answer
your letters myself.

Dear D.J.,

Thank you for my card. The wolf looks amazing!

You should see Pauline's bump. It's huge, and the baby's moving around now. Pauline let me feel its foot kicking. It felt really funny. Uncle Derek says she's so big there must be a football team inside her. As long as it's Liverpool!

Love, Max

P.S. We're doing lots of work on rhymes with Eggy. It's really difficult to find rhymes for some words. What would you rhyme with your name, 'Daphne'?

30th April

Dear Max,

Something to rhyme with Daphne...mmmm,
that's a difficult one! It would probably have to
be two words with one syllable each rather
than one word with two syllables. What about
something like 'splash me', or 'ash tree'. Ah,
now I've thought of one word with two
syllables – 'acne'. I'm not sure I should be
telling you that though in case you use it
against me!

I must go. I'm guest of honour at a charity
dinner tonight and I need to scrub up
my speech.

Love D.J.

There once was a writer called Daphne
Whose face was covered in Acne
She scrubbed it and scrubbed it
And rubbed it and rubbed it
Now it's smooth like the bark of an ash tree!
Mum says I can't send this, but I have!
Love Max

Dear Max

You are very cheeky! Have one back.

There was a young boy called Max
Whose body was made out of wax
In summer the heat
Started melting his feet
But in winter the cold froze his tracks.

       Love D.J.

P.S. Yours is better

8th May

Dear D.J.,

Just when I was feeling a bit better about everything, Mum's just told me that she and James have decided to buy a house together, and that they hope I will like the idea. I don't like the idea at all. I can't believe Mum wants to move from our flat. We've been here since Dad died and we've done it up ourselves and my bedroom is ace and I don't want to move. I ran up to my bedroom and slammed the door and refused to come down, especially when James came up to talk to me. Now I feel awful because I don't want to upset Mum, but I DON'T WANT TO MOVE.

Love, Max

10th May

Dear Max,

On the day I was supposed to move house for the first time (I was seven) I hid in the cupboard under the stairs because I didn't want to go, especially since I thought I wouldn't see any of my friends ever again. My parents had to lure me out with promises that I could have dinosaurs on the wallpaper in my bedroom and my own bit of garden where I could plant my own seeds.

I know you're a bit old for hiding in cupboards, but perhaps you could hide all the keys to the flat so the new people can't move in, or you could find out who the removal men are and ring up and cancel them.

Love D.J.

P.S. I was glad I moved in the end because the house was bigger and I had a bigger bedroom. If nothing else, hold out for a bigger bedroom!

Dear D.J.,

I sat down with Mum and we talked and talked and talked, but we're still going to move even though I told her I don't want to. Mum said we'll be able to move somewhere much bigger with a garden, but I bet she's only saying that to make me change my mind. I can go with them to look at all the houses and help to choose, but I don't really want to because it'll be boring and they'll think they can persuade me.

Ben thinks I should be excited because he likes moving house, and he said at least I'm not moving countries like he had to when he moved from Jamaica. Emily said at least I wouldn't be living so close to Jenny any more. That's the only good thing.

Love, Max

Dear Max,   20th May

Be positive, Max. You never know, you might find you like being in a new house, and you might even enjoy having James living with you. There's nothing like doing things man to man sometimes, like shouting at the football on the television. (Christopher does that, and I know he knows that I think he's off his trolley when he does.)

Talking about being positive, I'm going to make myself be positive about my writing block... I DO NOT HAVE WRITER'S BLOCK! I AM A GOOD WRITER AND I AM ABOUT TO START WRITING MY BEST BOOK YET! JUST YOU TRY AND STOP ME!

Love D.J.

Dear D.J.,

YOU'RE RIGHT. YOU DO NOT HAVE
WRITER'S BLOCK. YOU ARE THE BEST
WRITER EVER AND YOU ARE GOING TO
WRITE THE BEST BOOK EVER!

You'll never believe what happened, D.J. I was
on the bus going home
from school
and Huge
Bigbottom
came and sat
in the seat

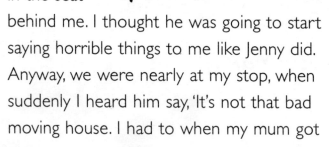

behind me. I thought he was going to start
saying horrible things to me like Jenny did.
Anyway, we were nearly at my stop, when
suddenly I heard him say, 'It's not that bad
moving house. I had to when my mum got

together with her boyfriend.' I looked round
a bit to see who he was talking to, and
I realised it was me. He looked me straight in
the face and said it again, 'You might prefer
your new house.' I had to get up to go then
and I just nodded. I didn't know what else to
do because I didn't know why he was saying it.

When I told Ben about it today, he said it
sounded as if Huge Bigbottom wanted to be
friends. Can you believe that?! I always thought
he hated me since I stood up to him in front
of everyone else. And then I thought about it
a bit more, and realised that he was telling me
as well that his dad isn't his real dad, like James
isn't my dad, even though I might be going to
live with him. I wonder what happened to
Huge's dad?

Love, Max

29th May

Dear Max,

What a turnaround for Huge Bigbottom.
I think Ben is right, he must want to show
a bit of solidarity with you.

I have written the first words of my new novel.
All 200 of them. Only another 39,800 or so to
go! At the moment it's called *Hopeless Harry*,
and it's going to be about a boy who always
gets everything badly wrong because he never
thinks before he acts. One day of course he'll
get something very major right, and that will
be a turning point in his life. It's going to be
very funny – I hope.

The only trouble is that, just as I've started it,

I've got to go back to Hollywood to have a talk with the screenwriters on *My Teacher's a Fruitcake* – in two days' time. I hope that doesn't cause another writing block.

Love D.J.

Dear D.J.,

Did you meet George Moony this time? You've been abroad a million times, and I've never even been abroad once! IT'S SOOOO UNFAIR! 😊

I like the idea of *Hopeless Harry*. What sort of thing is he going to get wrong? Is he going to fall off chairs and be rude to his teachers and get lost on his way home from school? That would be a really hopeless thing to do if he goes to school every day! Is he going to have any friends, or will everyone hate him because he's hopeless?

I've got to write a poem with ten lines for homework tonight. Every two lines have got to rhyme together. James said he'll help me if

I need help — I think he's staying because he's cooking dinner for us. He's quite a good cook, better than my dad, who couldn't cook for toffee, but not as good as Mum. Mum  says he's better than her, but I don't think so. Last time his mashed potato had lumps in it. Anyway, we don't need another cook. Mum's always done the cooking and she might not want James to take over.

Love, Max

P.S. Mum's put our flat up for sale. She says I've got to keep my bedroom really tidy so that I don't put off any buyers. I feel like leaving it in a total mess because I still don't want to move. And I don't want people poking around in my bedroom. We're going to look at a house this weekend. Boring.

Dear D.J.,

The house we went to see was AWFUL. Even James had to admit it. It smelt of poo! The kitchen looked as if it had never been cleaned,

and the garden was so overgrown I didn't even know it had a pond until the estate agent (Mr Blobby, I called him – which made Mum snigger) told us. James said we would have had to spend a fortune to make it all right. If they're all that bad, we won't be able to move – Yeh!

Love, Max

30 PENCIL DRIVE, WRITINGDOM, DJ1 0AU

7th June

Dear Max,

I'm back, at least I think I am. My body clock doesn't know whether it's going forwards or backwards.

The house you went to see sounds dreadful. When I last went house-hunting, I looked round a house where the owner kept sixteen cats and didn't let them outside, even though it had an enormous garden. There were litter trays everywhere, even in the bathroom. The house could have been beautiful with a bit of work, but I didn't think I'd ever be able to get the smell of poo out of my nose.

Now, you will have to break this to your

mother gently, but I did meet George Moony! He is twice as handsome in the flesh as on television and very charming. Enclosed with this letter you will find his autograph, which I asked him to sign for your mother. Make sure she is sitting down when you give it to her! My meeting with the screenwriters went very well and they are not planning to make too many drastic changes this time – though the teacher is still, of course, going to be a man.

Love D.J.

P.S. How's the poetry? You haven't sent me anything for a while.

Dear D.J.,

I did what you said and made sure Mum was sitting down when I gave her the autograph. She is over the moony (ha ha!). She's going to write to you herself to say thank you. James and I keep mocking her for being so potty about a film star.

We went to see another house.
Mr Blobby showed us
round again – Mr
Slobby Blobby with
the hairiest nostrils
I've ever seen and the
biggest wet sausage

handshake – yuk! The house was brand new and all the rooms were painted the same colour. I thought it was all right, and the bedroom I would have had was big. It didn't really have a garden, just a patch of gravel, but it had an extra room they said could be my own sitting room. Mum and James didn't like it though. They said it had no character and they want a proper garden and the walls were so thin you would be able to hear EVERYTHING through them.

Love, Max

P.S. We've started doing acrostics at school. Do you know what they are?

P.P.S. How's *Hopeless Harry?*

19th June

Dear Max,

Acrostics – mmm...what about...

B- Beware, he's coming
L - lumbering up the road
O - oodles of hair up his nostrils,
B - big sausage fingers
B - big sausage toes
Y - yukky blobby handshake

They're not as easy as they look, are they?
I remember doing a very rude one about a
teacher I didn't like. Unfortunately, the
teacher found it and I had to write 100 times
'I must always show my teachers'. I seem to

remember I was quite naughty at school.

Love D.J.

P.S. *Hopeless Harry* is having a terrible time!

Dear D.J.,

I bet you were VERY naughty at school,
because in lots of your books you have people
doing naughty things.

These people came to look
round our flat. Mum
nagged me like mad to
tidy up, then these
people walked in and
the boy dropped his
sweet papers all over
the floor. I hated him
going in my room
because it's private and he was
staring at my posters and drawings. I heard
him tell his mum that my room was too small
and he didn't like our flat and didn't want to

move there. I thought he had a cheek. I told Mum not to sell it to them even if they wanted it.

It's Mum's birthday in eight days' time. James wants us to think of something special we can do for her. I'm going to write her a long poem and James is going to do a drawing to go with it (I want him to because he's better than me), and then we're thinking of somewhere to take her. We'll probably invite Uncle Derek and Pauline as well.

Love, Max

P.S. I like 'oodles of hair up his nostrils'! Yuk!

Dear D.J.,

I've done my acrostic for Mum's birthday. This is it.

M – makes things better when things are bad
O – only thinks of others, never of herself
T – teaches me all the things I need to know
H – helps me with my homework when I
    am stuck
E – even watches me play football in
    the freezing cold
R – really rather Rare.
    There's nobody else like her.

Do you like the 'really rather rare'? We've been doing alliteration, where words all begin with the same letter.

We're going to go to an Italian restaurant for Mum's birthday treat. James has asked them to make a cake and they're going to bring it out as a surprise.

Love, Mad Marvellous Max

P.S. What sort of thing does Hopeless Harry do? Hey, you beat me to it. Hopeless Harry is an alliteration!

27th June

Dear Mighty Mister Max

Your mother will be tickled pink when she
reads your acrostic (funny word, isn't it?
Sounds like a disease!). As for going to an
Italian restaurant with two handsome young
men and having a special cake brought out to
her – what more can a woman ask for?!

Hopeless Harry is indeed an alliteration as well
as being – well – hopeless. He's just missed out
on going to the biggest party of the year
because he left one pair of shoes out in the
rain and the other pair was chewed by his
puppy because he didn't put them away when
he was told. I'm really enjoying writing about

him. My last book, *Where There's a Will*, was much more serious, so it's a refreshing change to be silly.

I've just heard that the film of *My Teacher's a Fruitcake* will be coming out at the end of next year, so I hope you won't think that you're too old by then to go and watch it!

Love Daft Duck Daphne

30th June

Dear Delightful Dizzy Daphne,

Mum's birthday was AMAZING. I had spaghetti carbonara – delicious. Mum got all tearful when she read my acrostic. James and I had to pat her on the head and tell her she was a soppy ape. Uncle Derek took photographs. I can't wait to see the one when the waiter brought Mum her birthday cake and we sang 'Happy Birthday'. Afterwards we went back to Uncle Derek's house. Scallywag was so excited he nearly bowled Mum over. I showed them some of the card games Marshmallow's been teaching me, except that Uncle Derek knew most of them already and kept winning. Pauline kept dozing off because the baby's getting bigger now and she says it wears her out. I thought it must be like carrying a sack of potatoes in your tummy and she said it was just like that.

Some more people came round our flat today. They had a little girl with them and she was the biggest pain ever. She kept picking our things up and putting them down in the wrong place. When she picked up a bronze tiger that was my dad's, Mum was so cross she asked the people to tell her to leave our things alone – and do you know what the man said? He said, 'She's not doing any harm, is she?' I don't think Mum will sell our flat to them even if they want it. I don't think we'll ever sell it anyway, so we'll have to stay here. ☺

Love, Max

P.S. When we played charades for a bit, I did a charade of *My Teacher's a Nutcase* and guess what – nobody guessed it. Doh!

Dear D.J.,

Guess what, guess what, GUESS WHAT. Last
night I went downstairs to get a drink and
I heard Mum and James talking about Barbados.
So I poked my nose round the door and said,
'What's happening in Barbados?' and James said,
'I'm going to take you and your mum to
Barbados, if you'd like to go that is. I think we
all need a break from house-hunting.' I must
have stood there with my mouth open,
because Mum told me I was catching flies, then
I said, 'Are you serious?' and James said he had
never been more serious in his life, and that
I can take a friend if I like.

We're going to
Barbados, D.J., in the
middle of August!

Can you believe that? We're going on a great big fat aeroplane all the way to Barbados for two weeks!

Love, Max

P.S. I can't wait to ask Ben if he can come.

P.P.S. Have you heard of cinquains? We're doing those for poetry now.

4th July

Dear Max,

If I had some steel drums I'd start playing them because I'm so pleased for you that you're going to Barbados. You deserve it, Max, and you've beaten me to it, because I've never been there. James is a superstar, even if his mashed potato is lumpy!

I can quite honestly say I have never heard of a cinquain. You'll have to teach me.

Love D.J.

P.S. I'm glad the birthday went well. Fancy no one guessing *My Teacher's a Nutcase!*

Dear D.J.,

Jenny's ruined everything again, just when everything was good. She saw James leaving our flat this morning when she was coming down from her flat, and she's been saying things at school about Mum sleeping with someone.

I told her to shut up and she called me a puny little weed who thinks he's special just because a famous author writes to him. Ben and Emily told her to leave me alone, but then she started on them as well. She called Emily a prissy little fairy and told Ben he should go back to where he came from. I couldn't believe it when she said that, because that's the most horrible thing to say. I went right up to her and told her that she should go back to where she came from — a poo-filled hole in the ground.

Eggy came in and asked what was going on, so Jenny told him what I'd said. He was really shocked and asked me why, but I couldn't say because I didn't want to repeat what Jenny had said about Mum and Ben and Emily.

He's given me 100 lines as a punishment. I've got to write 'I must not be unkind about my classmates'.

Love, Max

P.S. Huge Bigbottom talked to me again. He said that Jenny is trouble and I should keep out of her way. I nodded but I couldn't help thinking that he was trouble as well, because he used to be so horrible to me and I don't know why he's suddenly started speaking to me.

P.P.S. We've got to go and see another house tomorrow. Boring.

10th July

Dear Max,

You never know, perhaps Huge Bigbottom is growing into a nicer person as he gets older. If he carries on like this, you'll have to start calling him by his proper name again – if you can remember it!

I'm sorry Jenny's decided to raise her ugly mug again. What a thoroughly unpleasant little minx she is. What surprises me, Max, is that you haven't given her the Max treatment. You usually think up funny or rude names for people you don't like and that helps you to cope with them. What happened to the funny name for Jenny? What about a rude poem even?

Don't let her get you down, she's not worth it.

Love D.J.

Dear D.J.,

I hate James. We had a row and I never want to speak to him again. Mum's sent me to my room for being rude, but it's not fair because if James was a kid he would have been sent to his room as well. Just because I didn't like the food he cooked and didn't want to eat it, and I had a bad day at school anyway because Eggy told me off for calling Jenny an ugly pig — which she is.

J— just because he's a grown-up doesn't mean he's right.

A - always there when sometimes I wish he wasn't

M - makes me feel like I'm in the way

E- everything has changed since he met Mum.

S- sometimes he's OK.

I've just heard the front door go which means James has gone home, and now I feel guilty because it was my fault.

Love, Max

Dear D.J.,

The Max treatment coming up! Why didn't
I think of it? Thanks, D.J. I'm going to call Jenny
'Jenny Rotten' because her surname is Cotton.
I've written a limerick as well.

Jenny is not very nice
She's not made of sugar and spice
    She's full of big spiders
    That wriggle inside her
And a very large helping of lice

It's made me feel
so much better
writing that.

I forgot to say, Ben went wild when I asked
him if he wanted to go on holiday to Barbados

with us, especially because it's near his home country – Jamaica. He's almost as excited as I am. He's asked his parents and they've said yes. We can't wait.

Love, Max

P.S. I said sorry to Mum and to James.

17th July

Dear Max,

It takes a big person to say sorry, so well
done big Max, and I love the poem about
Jenny Rotten.

I'm off on my travels again next week,
to Canada this time, and Christopher is
coming with me. I'm doing a tour of
bookshops – signing copies of My *Teacher's
a Nutcase* – but we're going to stay on in
Toronto because we've never been there
before. Another postcard for your collection
will be winging its way to you.

Love D.J.

Dear D.J.,

We finished school today – YEH! It's only about three weeks now till we go on holiday. We've had to have loads of injections for going away. It didn't bother me because I'm used to them, but James is so scared of needles that he has to lie down when he has an injection in case he passes out!

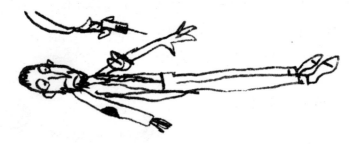

You'll never believe it but Hugo Broadbent (I'm not calling him Huge Bigbottom any more) has invited me to his birthday party! And Ben! We couldn't believe it when he gave us our invitations. He's having a disco in a church hall and he's invited lots of people (but not Miss Rotten). I found out from one of his friends that his dad isn't his real dad – his real dad left when he was a baby and Hugo hasn't seen him since, so he thinks of his new dad as his real dad. Perhaps that's why he's being friends with me, because he knows James isn't my real dad so we're a bit similar.

I still can't believe I'm going abroad again. I can't believe you're going abroad again either. I'm definitely, definitely, definitely going to be a writer when I grow up if it means I can go abroad all the time.

Love, Max

D.J.LUCAS

30 PENCIL DRIVE, WRITINGDOM, DJ1 0AU

23rd July

Dear Max,

Your letter has just plopped through the door,
so this is a quick one. We're off to the airport
in about an hour.

If you had told me two years ago that Huge
Bigbottom – sorry, Hugo Broadbent – would
one day be your friend, I would have curled up
in a ball with laughter. What a turnaround!

Don't be fooled into thinking that all writers
are rich, Max. Most struggle to make a living
from writing alone – I did for years. I'm one of
the lucky ones now: having a book made into
a film makes a big difference.

Love D.J.

P.S. Poor James. I know how he feels.

Dear D.J.,

Are you back? Did you have a good time?
Here's a welcome back cinquain for you.

It took me ages and ages and ages to write
because you have to obey all these rules about
numbers of syllables. It goes two, then four,
then six, then eight, then two. I'm really pleased
with it. I hope you like the picture as well.

Love, Max

4th August

Dear Max,

Yes, I'm back, and champing at the bit to continue with Hopeless Harry's hapless adventures. Your cinquain is brilliant. Here is my first ever attempt at one.

> Brave Max
> my biggest fan
> plays football like a star
> and writes poetry like a pote.
> Bravo!

I know, it's not as good as yours, and I'm cheating again, but the thought of a pote writing pomes made me giggle.

We had a wonderful time in Toronto relaxing after the first week of signings. It's a breathtaking city and the shops are – well, I'm sure you don't really want to know about the shops, but they are awesome.

I hope my postcard reaches you before you disappear on your own travels.

Love D.J.

Max
're having a fantastic time - lots
hard work and big dinners in the
rst four days, but lots of shopping an
uiet evenings alone in the second.
Christopher and I haven't been able
to spend so much time together
recently, so it's been good to catch up.
The picture on the front of this
card is of a moose (but you'll
know that). We didn't see one
but there are lots in some parts
of Canada. Strange how a
moose is so different from a
mouse, when there's only one
letter's difference in their names.
Love D.J.

30 Sharpener St
Anytown
MX9 3BT
U.K.

CANADA

TORONTO

9th August

Dear D.J.,

Cheat, cheat, cheat. Fancy a writer having to cheat to make a rhyme. 😊

I'm counting off the days till we go on holiday. I wish we could just flap our wings or click our fingers and be there. Ben's coming to stay the night before because we're leaving very early. I bet we don't sleep a wink. We might have to have a midnight feast! (Shhh!)

Hugo's disco party was cool. I gave him a CD (I chose it with James) and he seemed to really like it. There was a karaoke machine, and I did a song with Hugo and Ben and Emily. It was so bad everybody laughed (Ben can't sing in tune). I stayed at Ben's house afterwards

because Mum and James went to
a concert and were getting back
late. I like sleepovers. I didn't before
because I didn't want Mum to be on her own
in the house, but it's all right if James is with
her. Ben's got three cats and one of them slept
on my bed and chased my feet. I want to have
a cat but we can't in a flat (rhyme!).

Love, Max

P.S. Someone else came to look at our flat. The
estate agent thinks they're really interested in
buying it. I hope they do because I'm fed up
with having to keep my room tidy all the time.

P.P.S. Thank you for the postcard. Nice moose!

D.J.LUCAS

30 PENCIL DRIVE, WRITINGDOM, DJ1 0AU

11th August

Dear Max,

A quick note before you leave. Have
a wonderful, wonderful time, and don't
forget to send me a postcard. I shall be
waiting by the letterbox for it.

Love D.J.

D.J. It's amazing here! So HOT Colourful and busy. The people really friendly. I thought the food was a bit too spicy at first, but I'm getting used to it now. The beaches are really sandy and I can't believe how warm the sea is. I want to stay here for ever and ever. A steel band plays nearby every night. They let me and Ben have a go and it was brilliant. They also have limbo dancers. We had a go at that too but we were useless. James was better than us, and he's not good at sport! Say Hello to Hopeless Harry

Love Max

D.J. Lucas
30 Pencil Drive
Writingdom
DJ1 OAU
U.K.

Dear D.J.,

I'm back!!!!! We had such a brilliant time, D.J., and I'm nearly as brown as Ben (!). I loved it being hot all the time and I want to go back straightaway because it's raining here. The rain in Barbados is warm and sometimes it comes down in buckets, but it stops really quickly then the sun comes out again.

We had a villa with a shared swimming pool and two bedrooms, one for Mum and James (I didn't mind) and one for me and Ben. We went swimming every day, in the sea as well, and we had races with some of the other children who shared the pool. James is a really good swimmer, nearly as good as Ben. I'm getting better.

We did lots of eating out, and we went to a water park. It was even better than the one in Spain, with slides that started miles up in the air. Mum was too scared to go on them, so Ben and I went on with James.

James screamed louder than we did!

B - brilliant
A - amazing
R - really really amazing
B - beautiful
A - awesome
D - didn't want to come home
O - out of this world
S - sensational

Love, Max

P.S. Did you miss me?

2nd September

Dear Max,

I think I'd better catch the next flight out to Barbados, you've made it sound so wonderful. There's only one problem: *Hopeless Harry*. My publisher has moved the publication date forward because she doesn't want to miss out on the publicity there will be for *My Teacher's a Fruitcake*. So she wants me to finish it by the end of October so that it can come out next autumn. I can't blame her for putting the pressure on. I've had plenty of time. I just hope hopeless Daphne can sort Harry out quickly.

I've just finished a chapter where he manages to shut himself in a broom cupboard at the leisure centre, when he was supposed to be looking for the toilets. Nobody finds him for an hour and he misses his race at the swimming gala. Now, what's going to happen next...

Love D.J.

Dear D.J.,

The people I told you about want to buy our flat, but we haven't got anywhere to live yet so now we're going to have to look at houses all the time. We went to see three at the weekend. THREE! I don't know how anyone can have the patience to buy a house. I didn't want to go but Mum persuaded me because she said they wouldn't be able to choose without me. When I'm an adult I'll buy one place and stay in it for the whole of my life!

Two of the houses we saw were HORRIBLE. In the first one, the wallpaper was DISGUSTING and the carpets were BROWN with dirt. Mum said we could soon change the wallpaper and carpets, but I didn't want to live there. The second house was really cool. It had

a garden like
the one
we had
with Dad,
and the
bedroom
that would

be mine is twice as big as my one in the flat.
Mum said the kitchen was a bit small, but it's
bigger than the kitchen in our flat, and James
says he can make it bigger. He's good at
building because he's an architect. Somebody
else wants that house so we won't be able to
have it, and anyway James says it's too noisy
and he wouldn't be able to work in it, but it's
the only house I want. Then we saw a house
that I thought was TRULY horrible, but Mum
and James said they liked it the best! They said
it had lots of potential even though it was all
dilapidated and there was mould and damp
climbing up the walls and the wallpaper was
peeling off. James reckons he could turn it into

something special and that I could help. I think they've gone completely mad.

I go back to school tomorrow – bah! Some children change schools at my age, but we don't till we're thirteen. I don't know whether I'd prefer to change now or not. It feels a bit boring to keep going to the same school, but I think it would be frightening to go to a school you'd never been to before. I wouldn't mind as long as Ben and Emily came with me.

Love, Max

P.S. It's our birthdays soon. I'm going to be twelve!

6th September

Dear Max,

Thank you for reminding me about my birthday. I was trying to forget it!

There's another big occasion coming up – the Author of the Year Awards. I'm on the shortlist and I'm really excited about it. The award ceremony is on 3rd December and I shan't know who's won in advance, though I doubt very much it will be me because all the other shortlisted authors write for adults. Another new dress and shoes needed!

Hopeless Harry has fallen off a climbing frame and ripped a hole in the back of his trousers – and he doesn't know it's there.

So lots of people are giggling at him but he doesn't know why.

Love D.J.

P.S. Don't get too down about the house-hunting. I don't think your mother and James will buy anything that they can't turn into a palace, and you'll have fun helping them. I hope the new school term has started off well.

P.P.S. What sort of poetry will you be writing this term?

Dear D.J.,

Author of the Year – that's BRILLIANT!
Toes crossed.

We've got a new teacher.
His name's Mr Bloomer,
which is not a good name
for a teacher. He's rather
fat and he huffs and puffs
when he goes up and
down stairs, which you
have to a lot in our school.

He's a big fan of William Shakespeare and says
that Shakespeare is the greatest playwright
ever to have walked the earth, and that his
plays are sheer poetry. When I said I was a big
fan of D.J. Lucas, he said that he hadn't come
across you! Can you believe that, when you're

going to be Author of the Year?! That's the
second teacher I've had who hasn't heard
of you. I'm going to lend him *My Teacher's
a Nutcase* so that he can catch up.

Love, Max

P.S.

Look out William Shakespeare
I say.
I'm a fan of the writer D.J.
Her books are the greatest
Especially her latest
She'll be bigger than you are
one day!

Dear D.J.,

Pauline's had to go into hospital because she's got high blood pressure. Mum says that means that she needs to have lots of rest or she might become very ill and lose the baby. She went to visit her yesterday evening, and Marshmallow came to babysit with her boyfriend.

Her boyfriend is so tall he has to duck to come through the door. He's got an earring through his nose and five in each ear. I asked Mum if I could have one through my nose (I was only joking) and she said I could as long as I didn't mind if she had a tattoo across her forehead! Anyway, Marshmallow's boyfriend, Luke, is the best footballer I've ever seen in my life (even better than Uncle Twinkletoes!) and

he started teaching me how to do all
sorts of juggling skills with
the ball. Do you know, he
can flick the ball from his
foot onto the back of his
neck and it stays there?
I can't wait to be in the
football team again so that
I can show off. I was trying
to show Ben how to do
them today, and Hugo
came to watch. Then he
joined in, and he was better
than me.

Love, Max

P.S. Uncle Derek's coming for dinner tonight
because Mum says he won't eat if he's on his
own. Pauline's got to stay in hospital for at
least a week, so we'll be seeing a lot of Uncle
Derek. I hope that means we'll see lots of mad
Scallywag as well.

There once was a footballer called Luke
Whose skill with the ball was no fluke.
　He juggled and kicked it
　And dribbled and flipped it,
He was so good I called him the Duke.

13th September

Dear Max,

Great limericks, Max, and thank you for your
support. I don't think I'm quite in William
Shakespeare's league though! We owe an awful
lot of our language to good old William, but
I don't think people are going round quoting
from any of my books.

I'm sorry to hear about Pauline. How miserable
for her to have to stay in hospital. Please send
her my best wishes.

I'm enclosing your birthday card and
present – NOT to be opened until the 18th.
Christopher is taking me to Milan for three
days for my birthday. He says that if I need

dresses and shoes then that's the place to go.
Well, I'm not going to argue!

Love D.J.

To Max

A very happy
birthday

Love
D.J

D.J.

Happy Birthday

from your number one fan
who hopes you'll have an
awesome time

Love Max

19th September

Dear D.J.,

I can't believe you sent me all those DVDs!
Thank you soooooo much. I'll be watching
them forever (Mum and James want to watch
some of them too). I'm going to watch the
one about whales first, because whales are
my favourite.

Mum was sick yesterday morning, so my
birthday didn't start very well.
James made me a big
cooked breakfast
as a special treat,
while Mum
went back to
bed for a bit.

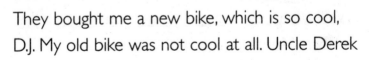

They bought me a new bike, which is so cool,
D.J. My old bike was not cool at all. Uncle Derek

and Pauline got me a CD player, which is really cool as well. My old CD player was not cool at all either.

Mum wasn't well again this morning. She thinks she must have a tummy bug.

Love, Max

Age 12!

P.S. Pauline's still in hospital but she hasn't had her baby yet. That means we won't have birthdays three days running – DOH! Uncle Derek doesn't know what to do with himself, he's so worried. He comes round to eat with us every night after he's been to visit Pauline and we try to cheer him up. It's getting quite crowded with James there as well, but I like it because we feel like a proper family again, even though James can never replace my dad. We'll be an even bigger family when the baby is born. Mum's really excited about it.

P.P.S. We're not doing poetry this year. We've gone back to writing stories, but I'll still write pomes ☺ sometimes. My stories will be even better now that I'm older. You just wait till they turn one into a film (starring Jude Flore!).

Saluti da Milano, Max,
This must be one of the noisiest
places on earth. The traffic is
horrendous - everyone driving
bumper to bumper and tooting
their horns non-stop. The Ice creams
though are to die for. I asked
for a large Ice cream and
was presented with a glass the
size of a goldfish bowl with
twelve scoops in it - much to
Christopher's amusement (and
the waiter's). I hope you had a
wonderful birthday.

Ciao D.J.

30 Sharpener St.
Anytown
MX9 3BT
U.K.

Dear Max

I'm back and with some very good news. At last, Max, there's a publication date for 'Dear Max'! I thought it would never happen. It's coming out on March 5th. next year.

Love D.J.

30th September

Dear D.J.,

Pauline's had her baby at last. Two weeks late! It's a boy and it weighs 8lb. Uncle Derek is so excited he can't sit down. He came over last night and told us all about it. He says the baby is the most handsome he's ever seen, and they're going to call him Benjamin. Can you believe that? I can't wait to tell Ben.

Mum and I are going to see Benjamin this evening.

I can't believe that *Dear Max* is going to be published at last. It's taken ages and ages and ages, and it's still another six months away. That's worse than waiting for Pauline to have her baby! I'm not sure I could be patient enough to wait that long if I was a writer.

Love, Max

3rd October

Dear Max,

Congratulations to Pauline and Uncle Derek on the arrival of Benjamin. They must be so relieved.

Yes, it can take an unbelievably long time for a book to be published. I've waited for four years before now, though not recently. Sometimes a book is delayed because the illustrator is too busy to start work straightaway, sometimes publishers have to juggle their programme so that they don't have too many books coming out at the same time, and there are all sorts of other reasons as well. Of course it can be frustrating though, because when you've written

137

something you want to see it in print as soon
as possible.

Love D.J.

Dear D.J.,

You're never going to believe what's happened.
Mum's going to have a baby. That's why she
kept being ill. She took me out for a pizza last
night and told me. She was all excited that
I was going to have a little brother or sister,
even though she said it was a bit of a surprise,
and she wanted me to be excited. But I didn't
want it to be true.

I STILL DON'T WANT IT TO BE TRUE. She
wants me to be happy but I'm not. It's just like
Jenny said when Mum and James first started
going out. She said if they had a baby together
I wouldn't be wanted as much.

It's going to be nothing but babies now –
babies, babies, BABIES.

Love, Max

P.S. I never want to see James again.

Babies
They make you ill.
They sleep and eat and poo.
They cry all day long and all night
Nappies

Relax Max   10th October

Fancy having a new baby brother or sister AND moving house. What an exciting time in your life.

You know that Miss Rotten is not a nice person, remember your poem? Why pay attention to anything she says?

Of course your mother and James will love you just as much, and you'll have all the fun of being the big brother.

I'm ten years older than my brother and I adored helping to look after him when he was tiny.

Be happy, Max. Big changes are always scary, but be positive and make the most of them.

You said you liked the feel of being a proper family again, and it would be pretty dull if nothing ever changed!

Love, D.J.

14th October

Dear D.J.,

Now Mum's told me that we're probably going to buy that horrible mouldy pigsty of a house that's the worst one we saw. I talked to Ben about Mum having a baby and moving house and we had a row because I didn't agree that it would be all right. Why does everyone think it will be all right when they're not in my life? Even Emily's being funny with me because she says I'm snappy. I deserve to be snappy.

Love, Max

15th October

Dear D.J.,

We've definitely sold our flat now so we'll
have to move, and Mum and James have put
in an offer on the pigsty. I don't believe James
when he says it will be great. It's so horrible
I won't be able to have any of my friends
round. We had a big row about it this
evening. He said I'm being difficult and making
Mum unhappy. I couldn't believe he said that.
I said he was the one making her unhappy by
making her move to a horrible house, then
I stormed up to my room. Mum's tried to
come in to talk to me, but I shouted at her to
go away and leave me alone. Now I feel awful
because we never have rows, but it's not my
fault that we're moving to a horrible house
and that she's having a baby.

Love, Max

20th October

Dear Max,

It's so hard to visualise what a house might look like when it's been left to rot, but it's also amazing to see what can be achieved. My architect completely transformed my cottage. How about challenging James to draw pictures of what the pigsty could look like? He's so good at drawing he should be able to give you a very good idea.

I've only got two weeks now to finish *Hopeless Harry*. He's in lots of trouble. He's dropped his mother's car key down a drain (accidentally) and he's flat on the ground with a coathanger trying to fish it out.

Love D.J.

Dear D.J.,

Mum and I had one of our long talks and everything's all right now. She says I'm going to be so important in helping with the baby and helping to make the new house nice. She says that when she's big and fat and tired with the baby, she'll be relying on me. I said sorry to James and he said sorry to me and that it's an exciting and difficult time for everyone. I asked him to do some drawings, and he's going to as soon as he has a moment.

Ben's still a bit funny with me, but Hugo sat next to me at lunch. He said that Miss Rotten was gossiping about my mum and that I wasn't to listen. He said that he's got a baby sister and he wouldn't swap her for anything, but he didn't like it when he knew his mum was going to have a baby and he took it out on everyone else, including me. That's amazing, isn't it?

Love, Max

P.S. Hugo passes to me at football all the time now. We've won our first five matches this term, which is a record.

28th October

Dear Max,

Good old Hugo, he's really coming up trumps.
I'll have to write a book about him at this rate!
Well done on the record streak of match wins.

I bet James's drawings for the pigsty will be
superb, and make sure you have your say
when it comes to your room. Just think, Max,
it's like having a blank canvas, you can start
completely from scratch and everything will
be new. You'll have so much fun choosing
paint colours and wallpaper and curtains.
In fact, it makes me feel like redecorating my
own cottage!

One more chapter to go on *Hopeless Harry*.
What sort of poetry are you doing at school
now, or have you moved on to something else?

Love D.J.

P.S. Hang on to your good friends, Max.
They're important people in your life.

31st October

Dear D.J.,

Mum and I have just come back from seeing

Benjamin again. He's so
tiny! He's not as
handsome as Uncle
Derek says. (I think he's
quite ugly, but don't tell
Uncle Derek.) Pauline
let me hold him and

I was really scared in case I dropped him. Uncle
Derek said it was good I could get some
practice in before I had my own baby to hold.

When we got home, James had cooked
a great big bowl of spaghetti bolognese, and
said we were celebrating. You'll never guess
what. We're going to be moving into the pigsty
on 20th December but I don't mind any more.

James has done some drawings and it's going to be AMAZING! My bedroom will be twice as big as the one I have now because we're going to pull a wall down. (James says I can help do that because it's only made of rubbish material.) I'm going to have my own sitting room as well. There's even a bedroom for the baby. I can't wait to move now!

Love, Max

P.S. You wait till Miss Rotten finds out. She'll be soooooo jealous, and she won't be able to spy on us any more.

B- baby boy
E- early into the world
N - noisy eater
J - joy for Uncle Derek and Pauline
A - amazingly tiny
M - mouth like a goldfish
I - eyes of blue, shut them tight
N - night night

3rd November

Dear Max,

I've finished *Hopeless Harry*, bang on time!
He's just saved his best friend from being run
over – pushed him out of the way just in time,
but broke his leg in the process! Now he's
a hero and all over the local papers.

That's such good news about the house,
Max. I'm sure you'll love it there once you've
settled in.

Christopher is whisking me off for some
sunshine for a few days before I give some
thought to my next project. We're going to do
nothing except lie on a beach, read and swim.
You'll have a postcard from Sardinia to add to
your collection.

Love D.J.

P.S. I like the acrostic. You haven't lost your touch – though I see you've learnt to cheat like me.

Dear Max

I am so relaxed I can hardly put pen to card. What more can we ask for than sun, sea and sand? I could stay here forever. Oh no, here comes trouble – Christopher demands that we go on a banana boat (like the one on the front of the card). Just when I thought I could have a doze by the pool. Ah well, off I go.

Love D.J.

30 Sharpener St.
Anytown
MX9 3BT
U.K.

Dear D.J.,

It's not long now till we move. I've been really busy. We've had to start packing up all our things. It's really difficult deciding which things can be put away for the time being and which ones  are still needed. I've thrown loads of things away – lots of old toys from when I was little and clothes that don't fit me any more because I'm SO BIG now. I'm keeping some toys for Benjamin for when he's bigger.

Benjamin is soooooo cute (he's not quite so ugly now). He opens his eyes and he grins a bit (Uncle Derek says that's because he's got wind!). He doesn't do much else though, apart from sleep and feed (and poo). Scallywag doesn't know what to make of him. He's a bit jealous I think, and Uncle Derek has to give him lots of attention.

I don't know whether I want a baby brother or a baby sister. I think a sister would be good because I could spoil her. A brother would probably spoil my games but I'd be able to teach him how to play football.

I hope you had a good time in Sardinia (I had to ask James where it was and he showed me on the atlas), and ta, ta, ta, ta, ta for the postcard.

Love, Max

17th November

Dear Max,

There's nothing like a bit of sun and sea to recharge the batteries. Believe it or not, while I was away, I was hit by an idea for my next book. Or, at least, the idea you gave me for a book has suddenly started taking off in my head. I'm going to write about elephants – my first book about an animal. It'll be a story about an orphaned elephant and how it survives. I shall start doing research now – using the internet! Christopher is going to show me how (I told you I'm a dinosaur).

At least now when I go to the Author of the Year Awards I shan't feel like a fraud.

Love D.J.

Dear D.J.,

You're the favourite to win! Mum showed me in the papers. They're taking bets on you. They say you deserve it because of all the books you've written, and the films, and the overall quality and variety of your writing.

We've been to see our pigsty two more times now. I can't wait to move, we're going to have so much SPACE. AAAANNNNDDDD, Mum and James said we can have a kitten! Yippee! That will be my first ever pet.

I've inspired you again, haven't I — about the elephants? What would you do without me?! I know a lot about elephants if you need any more help... In fact, I've got to write an animal story for homework. I think I'll write about

elephants as well, but my story will be about
a mummy elephant who is going to have a baby
and what all the other elephants think of it.

Love, Max

ear Author of the Year, DJ

YOU <u>WON</u>! That's amazing.
It's all over the newspapers
today. There's a picture of you
holding up your award and
looking totally shocked.
Well done, DJ.
            Love, Max

D.J. Lucas,
30 Pencil Drive
Writingdom
DJI 0AU

D.J.LUCAS

30 PENCIL DRIVE, WRITINGDOM, DJ1 0AU

5th December

Dear Max,

What an evening! I nearly fell off my high
heels when my name was read out and I had to
stand up. How I made it to the stage I really
don't know.

The biggest problem with winning such
a prestigious award is that it makes putting pen
to paper (or finger to computer key) even more
nerve-racking. There's such a lot to live up to.
Talking of fingers, I'm just about to begin my
tour of bookshops across the country – five
bookshops per week and home in between.
With all the publicity from the film and last
night, I imagine my fingers will be ready to
drop off by the time I've finished signing.
I love doing it though. It makes me feel very

honoured when someone asks me to dedicate
one of my books to them.

Love D.J.

8th December

Dear D.J.,

It's my turn to tell you something exciting. I've won a prize at school – for creative writing! I did my story about the mummy elephant, and Mr Bloomer gave me a top mark. He said it was a very imaginative and descriptive piece of writing. (I hope your elephant story will do just as well, though I expect you haven't started it yet because of the tour.)

It means that I'll be going up on stage to collect my prize and shake hands with some important people at our Achievement Evening. (I shall be soooooo nervous. It's just as well I don't wear high heels because I would fall off them!) Emily's won the maths prize (she's SO clever), Ben's won the athetics prize and Hugo's won the football prize. So you're the

Author of the Year and I'm the Author of Our School(!)

Love, Max

P.S. I'll have to go and buy myself an outfit ☺

P.P.S. We're all packed up and nearly ready to move. The flat looks so empty without any pictures on the walls and no photos and bits and pieces anywhere. It looks a bit sad and makes me feel sad.

11th December

Dear Max

Fantastic, Max! It's your
turn to be the star. I wonder
if I could persuade your school
to lay out a red carpet for
you. Seriously, I am so
thrilled for you. I'll have to
watch out. My elephant
story might not be as good
as yours. Perhaps I'd better
write about something else!
Good luck, Max, and enjoy
your special evening.

Love D.J.

Dear D.J.,

THANK YOU, THANK YOU, THANK YOU!
Yesterday was the best day of my life, and it
was the best day of Ben's life and Emily's life
and Hugo's life (and the chocolate cake was
the best in anybody's life!). I can't believe that
you managed to keep it a secret that you
were presenting the prizes! I nearly fell off my
chair when you came on the stage, and Mum
kept nudging me. They were all talking about it
in school today, and they
thought it was so funny that
you curtseyed to me. Mum
said she had tears in her
eyes. She says you're even
nicer than she imagined
and she loves your red
shoes. (I think James

might buy her some red shoes for Christmas because she wants to be more daring with her clothes, even though she's having a baby.) Thank you too for taking us out afterwards. It made me feel like a superstar being with you because loads of people recognised you.

I wanted to ask that waiter if he wanted my autograph as well when he asked for yours. ☺ Mum's going to write to you as well, and so are Ben and Emily and Uncle Derek and

Pauline. Mum's going to send you our
new addresses.

I'm so lucky!

Love, Max

P.S. Last day of school tomorrow, and then
we move the day after. Yippee! Can't wait
for Christmas.

20th December

Dear Max,

That was the most wonderful evening I have
had for a very long time, and I'm so glad it
was such a surprise for you. You and your
family and friends are just as I imagined, and
I enjoyed every minute of your company. It
was so brilliant to meet at last after three years
of writing letters to each other.

You have such an exciting year ahead of you,
Max. New house, new baby, new kitten, new
stories to write – enjoy every moment, you
deserve it. As for me, elephants will rule for
the first part of the year, then there'll be all the
build-up to the new film.

Have a wonderful Christmas, and I hope the enclosed will add to the festive cheer in your new house.

Love D.J.

Daphne
Wonderful writer
Max her number one fan
Met at last over choccy cake.
Perfect.

Dear D.J.

Happy Christmas D.J.

Love
Max

Have you read the other Max books?

ISBN: 1 84362 383 8   £4.99

Don't miss the first story
about Max.

ISBN: 1 84362 691 8   £4.99

And look out for the
second book too!

More Orchard Red Apples

Orchard Red Apples are available from all good bookshops, or can be ordered direct
from the publisher: Orchard Books, PO BOX 29, Douglas IM99 1BQ
Credit card orders please telephone 01624 836000
or fax 01624 837033 or visit our Internet site: www.wattspub.co.uk
or e-mail: bookshop@enterprise.net for details.

To order please quote title, author and ISBN
and your full name and address.
Cheques and postal orders should be made payable to 'Bookpost plc.'
Postage and packing is FREE within the UK
(overseas customers should add £1.00 per book).

Prices and availability are subject to change.